PONY PARADE

Also in the Animal Ark Pets series

LUCY DANIELS
Pony Parade

Illustrated by Paul Howard

*Hodder
Children's
Books*

a division of Hodder Headline plc

Special thanks to Pat Posner

Text copyright © 1997 Ben M. Baglio
Created by Ben M. Baglio, London W6 0HE
Illustrations copyright © 1997 Paul Howard
Cover illustration by Chris Chapman

First published in Great Britain in 1997
by Hodder Children's Books

A Catalogue record for this book is available from the British Library

ISBN 0 340 68731 2

Typeset by Avon Dataset Ltd, Bidford-on-Avon, Warks

Printed and bound in Great Britain by
Mackays of Chatham PLC, Chatham, Kent

Hodder Children's Books
a division of Hodder Headline plc
338 Euston Road
London NW1 3BH

Contents

1

James on holiday

"Come on, Blackie," Mandy said. She smiled down at the young Labrador and tugged gently on his lead. "We'll have to turn round and go back now. They'll be waiting for you!"

Blackie wagged his tail and carried on snuffling at the grass verge. "Come *on!*"

Mandy said more firmly. "You've sniffed enough to last for hours. Besides, here's James coming to fetch us," she added as she saw her best friend running down the lane.

"Hurry up, Mandy," James called. "We're almost ready to leave."

Blackie looked up at the sound of James's voice. Then, barking joyfully, he tugged Mandy off towards him.

"Well, *that* got him moving!" Mandy chuckled, handing Blackie's lead to James.

"Good job too," James said. "Mum and Dad are just loading the last lot of stuff into the car. Gosh, Mandy, there are so many bags. You'd think we were going for a month, not just three days!"

Just then Blackie started pulling at the lead and James groaned. "Not that way, Blackie. Back home quickly, boy. Dad won't want to be kept waiting. Oh, help!" he added. "Now he's wound his lead round my legs."

Mandy bent to unwind the lead. As soon as she'd done it, Blackie jumped up at her and nearly knocked her over. "What a pest you are, Blackie," she said lovingly. "Now, get walking!"

"That's what he was like before you came and took him out," James said as, at last, Blackie started walking in the right direction. "Getting in everyone's way, tripping us up or almost knocking us over. *And* he kept pulling things out of boxes and running off with them."

"He probably thought he was helping," Mandy chuckled.

"That's what *I* said," James told her. "But Mum and Dad didn't agree."

"Poor Blackie," Mandy said, bending to stroke him. Blackie sat down suddenly and James almost fell over him.

"Whoops!" Mandy laughed. "Sorry, James. That was my fault."

They straightened themselves out and started walking again.

"Here you are," said Mr Hunter as they reached the car. "You've been so long I thought you'd taken Blackie home, Mandy. Imagined you'd decided to keep him with you while *we* went on holiday," he joked. The Hunters were having a long weekend in the Lake District.

"I wish I could," Mandy replied. "I'm really going to miss him." She bent to give the Labrador a final pat. Then James put him in the back of the car, behind the special dog guard.

"*I'm* going to miss Benji," James said. "Look, he's sitting on the wall, watching. I'm sure he's upset about being left behind."

"James! If you don't get in, we'll leave *you* behind, as well," said Mrs Hunter, popping her head out of the car window. "Stop worrying about Benji. He'll be fine with Mrs Padgett looking after him."

Mrs Padgett was the Hunters' next-door neighbour. She loved cats and Benji was very fond of her.

"Yes, I suppose you're right," James said as he scrambled into the car. "OK, Dad. I'm ready!"

"Bye, James!" Mandy called as the car set off. "Have a great time. I'll see you in three days!"

Mandy waved until the car turned the corner. Then she turned to look at Benji. She was just in time to see his tail disappearing round the side of Mrs Padgett's house. So Benji didn't seem to mind about being left behind, after all!

Mandy smiled and set off for home. She lived at the other end of the village from James in an old stone cottage called Animal Ark. It was a good name. Mr and Mrs Hope, Mandy's parents, were vets and their surgery was attached to the house.

There was only one car parked outside Animal Ark when Mandy got there, which meant morning surgery was nearly over. Mandy recognised the car. It was Mrs Todd's.

Mrs Todd was Mandy's teacher. She had a spaniel called Jodie. Mandy was just wondering what was wrong with Jodie when Mrs Todd came out of the surgery door. Jodie was prancing happily at her side. Mandy smiled; there didn't seem to be much wrong with her at all.

"Hello, Mandy," said Mrs Todd. "Jodie's just had her booster injection."

"Hello, Mrs Todd," Mandy replied as she bent down to stroke the spaniel. "I was a bit worried when I saw your car

here. I'm glad there isn't anything wrong
with her."

Mandy petted the lively dog for a few
seconds. Then she looked up at her
teacher. "Are you enjoying your holiday,
Mrs Todd?" she asked.

"Yes, thank you. I am," Mrs Todd
replied. "But there isn't much left of it
now. Just over a week to go."

"I know." Mandy nodded her head.

"Mum's taking me into Walton to get some new school shoes this afternoon."

"No James today, then?" Mrs Todd wasn't James's teacher. James was eight, a year younger than Mandy and in a different class. But Mrs Todd knew they were best friends.

"He's gone away for three days with his mum and dad," Mandy said, looking sad. "They'll be staying in a caravan so they've taken Blackie with them. I'm starting to miss them already and I've only just seen them off!"

"Never mind, Mandy," said Mrs Todd with a kind smile. "Three days isn't long. They'll be back before you know it."

"I suppose so," Mandy replied. "I bet Blackie will get up to all sorts of mischief in the caravan. And on the beach," she added. "James will have loads to tell me when he gets back."

"I expect you'll have a lot to tell James as well, Mandy. Just you wait and see," said Mrs Todd.

Mandy smiled. Mrs Todd was right. Three days wasn't long. Not really. She'd have to find plenty of things to do to stop her from missing James and Blackie too much.

2

A new friend

"Hi, Jean," Mandy said, standing on tiptoe to peer over the reception desk. "Wow! What happened?"

Jean Knox, Animal Ark's receptionist, was kneeling on the floor surrounded by a sea of paper, envelopes and postcards.

"Hi, Mandy!" Jean glanced up. "Mrs

Todd's Jodie happened, that's what! She jumped up at the desk to say hello to me and managed to knock everything off."

"Sounds like the sort of thing Blackie would do," Mandy said. She went round to help Jean sort out the mess.

"You can put these postcards into their envelopes if you like," Jean said. "They're reminders, to let people know that their pets are due for a booster injection. They were all in order until Jodie knocked them down. You'll have to sort them out carefully, though. Make sure you put the correct card in each envelope."

"Or Mrs Stafford might wonder why she's been asked to bring Rover to Animal Ark when she's got a cat called Pixie!" Mandy chuckled.

"I see you're back from seeing James off, Mandy!" Mrs Hope's head appeared over the desk. "But what *are* you two doing down there?" she added.

"Hi, Mum," Mandy said. "Jodie knocked everything on to the floor. I'm

helping Jean to put the reminder cards into their envelopes."

"That's good," Mrs Hope said. "I've just got one or two house calls to make before lunch. Dad should be back at about two o'clock. We'll go and get your new shoes then, Mandy."

"Where is Dad?" Mandy asked.

Mrs Hope smiled. "He's up at Giants Farm doing some blood tests on Mr Grove's cows."

Mandy giggled. It always made her laugh when she thought of Mr Grove living at Giants Farm. He was such a small man! His farm was called Giants Farm because it was near a huge rock called the Giant's Seat.

"Oh, Mandy, Gran phoned to see if you wanted to go round for tea," Mrs Hope added. "I said we'd call in at Lilac Cottage on our way back from Walton."

"Great!" said Mandy. "I can't wait to find out if the new people have moved in yet!"

"Well, you haven't got long to wait now," Jean said with a smile. She handed Mandy a few envelopes. "There, I think that's all of them."

"Yup!" Mandy checked the floor, then dragged a chair over to Jean's small desk and set to work.

"I hope it rains soon," Mandy said to her mum. They were on their way back from Walton. And, as well as her school shoes,

Mandy also had a new pair of wellies. She couldn't wait to wear them.

Mrs Hope laughed. "Don't let the farmers hear you wishing for rain, Mandy. Not until they've got their harvest in!"

"Grandad would like it to rain," Mandy said. "He told me that the hot, dry weather makes gardening hard work. Oh, look," she added, "there's a car outside Jasmine Cottage. The new people must have moved in. Drive a bit slower, Mum. I want to see if I can see anyone."

Mandy twisted in her seat to get a better look. "Nope," she said. "But they *have* moved in. There's curtains up in the windows."

"I expect Gran will be able to tell you all about them," said Mrs Hope as she pulled up outside Lilac Cottage. "She's sure to have welcomed them to Welford."

"Gran met them when they came to look at the cottage," said Mandy. "She said there's a boy a bit younger than me. I don't know if he's got any pets, though."

"I'm sure you'll find that out soon enough!" Mrs Hope chuckled, then added, "Here's Gran now."

Mandy jumped out of the car and ran up the garden path. "Hi, Gran. Just wait until you see my new wellies!"

"Hello, Mandy, love. I wasn't expecting you so soon. I was just going to take these tomatoes round to Mrs Jackson."

Grandad popped his head out of the greenhouse door, chuckling. "I expect you could persuade Mandy to take them for you, Dorothy."

Mandy laughed. She ran over to give Grandad a hug. "You bet I will!" she said.

Mrs Jackson lived two doors away from Lilac Cottage. Her cottage was called Rose Cottage. Every summer the grey stonework was almost hidden by the roses that climbed up every wall and around the doors and windows.

Mrs Jackson's daughter, Jane, had a pony called Prince. Mandy loved all animals but Jane's pony was one of her special favourites. She nearly always went to see him when she visited her grandparents.

"And I bet you'd like a nice carrot for Prince," Grandad said. "I've just dug some up for your mum to take home. Come and choose one; then we'll give it a rinse under the garden tap."

A few minutes later Mandy went off with the bag of tomatoes and a juicy carrot. An unfamiliar boy was running along ahead of her. She wondered if he was the new boy from Jasmine Cottage.

Suddenly, he tripped up and fell to the ground with a thump.

Mandy gasped and ran to catch up with him. "Are you OK?" she asked, kneeling down beside him. "Have you hurt yourself?"

"I banged my knee really hard!" he said. He rolled over into a sitting position

and peered at it. "I think I landed on a stone or something," he added. "It's just scraped. I'll be OK when it stops stinging."

"Where were you going in such a hurry?" Mandy asked.

The boy looked up and smiled. "There's a fantastic pony in the orchard here. I was on my way to see if he'd make friends with me."

"He's called Prince," Mandy told him. "He is a lovely pony and I'm sure he'll make friends. But I think you should get your knee seen to first. Look, it's bleeding, and you've got some dirt in it."

"Is that you, Mandy?" a voice called from behind the thick, high hedge.

"Yes it is, Mrs Jackson," Mandy called back. "And . . . what's your name?" she asked the boy.

"I'm Paul Stevens," he told her. "We've just moved in to Jasmine Cottage."

"And Paul from Jasmine Cottage is here, too, Mrs Jackson. He's hurt his knee."

"Well, you'd better bring him in, Mandy. I'll meet you at the gate."

Mandy picked up the bag of tomatoes. Then she and Paul walked to Mrs Jackson's gate. Mrs Jackson looked down at Paul's knee. "It doesn't look too bad," she said. "Come on, we'll go indoors and ask Jane to bathe it for you."

"I was running to look at the pony," Paul said as they went up the garden path.

"I love ponies. And dogs and cats and things as well."

"You and Mandy will find plenty to talk about, then," Mrs Jackson said. She opened the back door and called out for Jane.

"Jane's fifteen. She's going in for nursing when she leaves school," Mrs Jackson told Paul as Jane got the first-aid box down. "She loves opportunities like this. She's always wanted to be a nurse."

"Just like I've always wanted a pony," Paul said. "And now we've come to live in Welford, I'm getting one! That's why I was coming to see *your* pony. I wanted to tell him all about it. I couldn't tell anyone else 'cos I don't know anyone here yet."

"Well, you know us now," Mandy said. "You can tell us all about it."

3
Exciting plans

"There," Mrs Jackson said proudly. "Jane's made a nice neat job of your knee, Paul. Does it feel better now?"

Paul ran his fingers over the strip of plaster Jane had put on the graze. "Yes, thank you, it does!" He nodded and slid off the high stool Jane had sat him on.

"How about a nice drink of rosehip cordial?" Mrs Jackson asked.

"Um . . ." Paul looked across at Mandy.

Mandy laughed. "I think Paul's longing to see Prince," she told Mrs Jackson. "And I'm dying to hear about the pony he's getting! Maybe we could have something to drink afterwards?"

"We'll put the drinks on a tray and take them to the orchard with us," Mrs Jackson said, her eyes twinkling merrily. "*I* want to hear all about Paul's pony, too!"

"Brilliant!" Paul said and dashed to the door. "Come on, Mandy!"

"Go on, you two," Mrs Jackson told them. "I'll catch you up with the drinks."

Paul certainly seems to like ponies! Mandy thought as they dashed along to the orchard. She felt sure she was going to like him – and that James would too!

Mandy loved the smell of the different fruits when the sun was shining down on them. The trees grew at either side

22

of the orchard behind fences made of rosewood. Prince couldn't reach the apples, pears and plums that weighed the branches down – he grazed happily and safely in the rest of the orchard.

Jane gave a whistle and the little Welsh pony trotted eagerly towards them.

"I won't be able to do that with my pony," Paul sighed, holding his hand out for Prince to smell it.

"Oh, you will, Paul," Jane told him. 'It doesn't take long for a pony to recognise a whistle."

Paul rubbed Prince's soft nose and looked glum. "But I *can't* whistle!" he blurted out.

"No problem," Mandy said. "My friend James is excellent at whistling. I'm sure he'll teach you when he comes home, Paul!"

Paul cheered up immediately. Mandy broke her carrot in two and handed him a piece. "Here," she said. "Give it to Prince. He loves carrots."

Prince's velvety nose twitched as Paul held the carrot out. His top lip moved as though he were smiling, then he moved his mouth closer to Paul's hand. Paul chuckled as Prince gently took the carrot. "He tickled my fingers!" Paul said in delight. "I *knew* he was a fantastic pony the minute I saw him! Oh, I hope mine will be as nice!"

Mrs Jackson arrived just then, carrying a tray with four tall glasses of bright-pink rosehip cordial.

"Right, Paul. Tell us about this pony before you burst!" she said as she handed out the glasses.

"Well," Paul said, his eyes shining brightly. "Someone came round from the Horse and Pony Rescue Sanctuary in Glisterdale this morning to look at our paddock and stable. They wanted to talk to us to make sure we were the right sort of people to give one of their ponies a home!" He stopped to catch his breath. But Mandy couldn't wait to hear the rest.

"And?" she said excitedly. "What did they say?"

"They said yes!" Paul grinned happily. "And . . . we're going to the sanctuary tomorrow to choose one!"

Prince nuzzled Paul's ear and whinnied softly. Everyone laughed.

"Prince thinks it's terrific news!" Jane said.

"It is, isn't it!" said Paul, stroking Prince's silky neck. "I can hardly wait for tomorrow!"

"You ought to ask Mandy to go with you, Paul," said Jane. "Her mum and dad are the local vets, so she knows quite a bit about animals."

Mandy smiled. She wasn't allowed to help with the sick animals who came to Animal Ark, but her mum and dad told her all about their illnesses and what they were going to do to make them better. And Mandy had read every single one of the pamphlets in the waiting room on caring for animals.

"Would you, Mandy?" said Paul. "Would you come with us?"

"Wow! *Would* I!" Mandy laughed. "But I'd better check it out with my parents first. My mum's at Gran and Grandad's – they live just up the road at Lilac Cottage."

"Let's go and ask now!" said Paul. He finished his drink in one gulp then wiped his hand across his mouth. "That was delicious, Mrs Jackson. Thank you."

"Yes!" Mandy agreed. "Thanks."

"Off you go then," Mrs Jackson said. "And thank your gran and grandad for the tomatoes, won't you, Mandy?"

"I will!" Mandy said. "Bye, Prince. We'll come and see you again soon."

"Yes, we promise," said Paul. Then he and Mandy hurried off.

"As soon as you get your pony and it's settled in, Paul, let me know. Then I can come round to see it!" Jane called out after them.

"Look, Mandy!" Paul said when they reached Lilac Cottage. "That's my mum in the garden with your gran and grandad! Is the lady with red hair your mum?"

"Yup!" Mandy nodded. "It seems our mums have already got to know each other!" The children dashed up the garden path.

"I see you and Paul have already met, Mandy!" her mum said. "Hello, Paul. I'm Mrs Hope."

"Hello," Paul replied breathlessly. "Mum, this is Mandy. And . . . and . . .

please can she come with us tomorrow to help choose my pony?"

The grown-ups looked at one another and laughed.

"What's the matter?" Mandy and Paul said together.

"Paul's mum has just been asking if Dad or I would go to the sanctuary with them to check over the pony they choose," Mrs Hope explained to Mandy. "We'd already fixed for you to come, too!"

4

The sad pony

Next morning, the Stevenses came to pick Mandy up straight after breakfast. She'd agreed to travel with them; Mrs Hope was going in her own car in case she got any emergency calls.

Mandy got in the back of the car with Paul. "Hi, Mandy," he said excitedly.

"We've got to keep an eye on the horse box for Dad. He isn't used to towing one. It isn't ours; we hired it when the sanctuary people said we'd be able to bring our pony home right away! Gosh, I can't wait to get there!"

"Paul!" Mrs Stevens laughed. "You're like a runaway train!"

Mandy laughed too. "But it's so exciting, Mrs Stevens. I can't wait either."

It wasn't a very long journey to Glisterdale, but to Mandy and Paul the ride seemed endless. At last they saw the sign for the Horse and Pony Rescue Sanctuary and Mr Stevens turned off the main road.

"These fields must belong to the sanctuary," said Mandy. "Look, there's loads of ponies grazing and wandering around and . . . Oh, look, Paul! There's a big cart-horse and some donkeys, too!"

Mrs Stevens twisted in her seat. "We're not having a donkey or a cart-horse,

Paul," she said teasingly. "Only a pony."

"I know, Mum." Paul chuckled. "Only a pony! But I do like donkeys," he added.

"Well, here we are," Mr Stevens said.

Paul gulped as the car drew to a stop. "I feel all funny inside, now we're really here," he said.

Mandy laughed. "You'll soon feel OK when you start looking properly at the ponies," she told him.

The sanctuary manager came out of a near-by stable block to greet them. "That's where we keep the newest arrivals," she told them. "There's a large run-out area at the back of the stables so they can go outside whenever they like. We keep them separate from all the others for a few weeks to give them a chance to settle in."

"And in case they've got something the others can catch?" Mandy asked.

The manager nodded. "There speaks the daughter of a vet," she said, smiling at Mrs Hope.

"Well we won't look at the ones in the stable block, then," said Paul. "It would be *ages* before I could have one of them!"

The manager smiled again. "Come on," she said, "I'll take you to the paddock where we keep the ponies who *are* ready to go to a new home. It's only just down here."

They followed the manager along a wide gravelled path with fields either side. Mandy saw some foals playing together. She'd have liked to have a closer look but she knew Paul wouldn't want to stop.

But suddenly, he *did* stop. He was staring at a brownish-grey pony in one of the fenced-off fields. The pony was a few metres away from the fence and was looking straight at Paul.

Mandy's heart lurched. The pony had such sad, sad eyes that peered out from under a dull, heavy fringe of dark-brown hair. One eye looked smaller than the other and Mandy realised it was a bit swollen and puffy underneath. His coat was dull too, and his ribs stuck out. He was really thin and Mandy caught her breath when she saw a few nasty-looking sores, and the scars and patches that covered the pony's back and sides.

The pony started moving very slowly towards the fence. His eyes seemed to be fixed on Paul. Mandy heard Paul take a deep, wobbly breath. Then he crept delicately up to the fence.

Paul and the pony arrived at the fence at exactly the same moment. For a split second they just stared at each other. Then the pony whinnied softly and laid his big broad head on Paul's shoulder.

"My word!" said the sanctuary manager. "That's the first noise Paddy's made since he came here. And it's the first time he's *ever* wanted to make friends with anyone! He's such a sad pony!"

Paul held his hand out for Paddy to sniff. Then, carefully and gently, he stroked the pony's greyish muzzle. Paddy

breathed heavily and made a soft whickering noise. When Paul stopped stroking him, the pony pushed his face into Paul's neck.

"He's asking you to stroke him again," whispered Mandy, coming to stand close to Paul.

"I don't have to choose a pony!" Paul said. "Paddy's chosen *me*!"

But the sanctuary manager shook her head. "I think Paddy will have to be one of our permanent residents," she said. "We rescued him a few months ago from someone who'd treated him very badly indeed."

She walked quietly forward and pointed to the scars on Paddy's back. "These are from where he'd been whipped," she explained. "He was covered in nasty sores, he was starving and his left eye was bruised and swollen. His eye isn't quite right yet and we bathe it twice a day for him. The scars will fade a little bit more in time but we still have to put special ointment on some of them. They were worse than all the others and are taking longer to heal."

"But I could do all that if you showed me what to do," said Paul. "Mandy would help me, wouldn't you, Mandy?"

Mandy nodded. "And I'm sure James would as well," she said.

"Paul, I really think you should look at some of the other ponies," Mrs Stevens said. "I'm sure you'll see one you like."

"I won't see one I like as much as Paddy!" said Paul. "Paddy's special. He chose me and . . . and look! He *trusts* me."

Paddy's head was resting on Paul's shoulder again. The scarred pony's eyes were half-closed and his body was swaying gently. Mrs Stevens moved over to them and stood behind Paul to look at Paddy. The pony blew softly into her face.

"See, Mum. Paddy likes you, too," Paul said.

"What do you think now you've seen them together?" Mrs Stevens asked the manager.

"Paddy does seem to have taken to your son," the manager replied thoughtfully. "And he blew at you. That's a sign of friendship. He certainly didn't want to be friends with any of us. I think maybe we *shouldn't* dismiss it out of hand. Paul's right. The pony does seem to trust him. That would help enormously in getting Paddy *properly* better. But Paul would have a lot of hard work in front of him."

Paul looked pleadingly at his mum and dad.

"Let's ask Mrs Hope to examine Paddy and see what she says," suggested Mr Stevens. His wife nodded.

Mrs Hope had a few quiet words with the sanctuary manager and Paul's parents. Mandy and Paul stood by Paddy, petting him and talking to him. Then the manager hurried away towards one of the buildings.

"Right, Paul," Mrs Hope said. "The manager has gone for a bridle and leading rein. We're going to see if Paddy will let you lead him around the field. If he does, I want to watch carefully to see how he moves and behaves. Then, if everything there seems OK, I'll give him a good checking-over."

The manager came back and fixed on the leading rein. "All right, Paul. Come into the field now," she said quietly.

"Don't go behind Paddy," Mandy whispered. "Let him see you walking towards him, Paul."

"I know you shouldn't walk up behind ponies," said Paul. "I had some riding lessons where we used to live."

"Go on, then!" Mandy smiled. "And good luck." She wished she could go into the field and walk with Paddy and Paul. But Mandy knew that it was something Paul had to do by himself. She moved over to stand next to her mum, crossed her fingers and watched anxiously.

Paddy behaved really well. He seemed to enjoy walking along beside Paul. Paul led him right to the other end of the field.

A road ran past the end of the field and Mandy held her breath when a very noisy motor-bike whizzed by, close to the hedge. But Paddy stayed calm and quiet.

"He heard it, though," Mrs Hope murmured. "I saw his ears pricking forward. I think he could be an Exmoor pony. They can be nervous."

"Oh, I don't want Paul to have a nervous pony," said Mrs Stevens, looking worried.

"No, no, I don't think Paddy is," Mrs Hope told her. "We'll see how he behaves when I examine him."

"You mean you think Paddy's OK so far, Mum?" Mandy asked.

Mrs Hope smiled. "Maybe. But let's wait and see."

When Paul brought Paddy back up to Mrs Hope, she told him to come out of the field. "You can watch from this side of the fence while I examine him," she added with a smile.

"OK," Paul replied. "But how long will it take?" He looked very anxious.

"Not too long, but I expect it will seem like a long time to you."

Paul and Mandy watched as Mrs Hope looked in Paddy's eyes and his mouth. She listened to his heart and chest, and ran gentle fingers over his body and down his legs.

Mandy held her breath when her mum picked up one of Paddy's feet. She knew ponies often didn't like that. Paul seemed to know, too, because he was holding on tight to the fence post.

But Paddy didn't seem to mind. When Mrs Hope picked up one of his back feet, he even turned his head to nibble gently at the top of her hair.

At last, Mrs Hope finished. She patted Paddy and climbed nimbly over the fence. "Well," she said, "considering what Paddy's been through, he's really quite healthy. His coat should improve with a lot of hard work and attention, and his scars will fade eventually."

Mandy nudged Paul and showed him her crossed fingers. Paul nodded. His fingers were crossed, too.

"He *is* an Exmoor pony," Mrs Hope added. "He's got seven molar teeth. Only Exmoors have seven."

"You said Exmoors could be nervous," said Mr Stevens.

"Mmm." Mrs Hope nodded thoughtfully. "The breed takes its name from the high, wild moorland in the south-west of the country. There are still more or less untamed herds running on Exmoor and they don't have much contact with humans. But some of the ponies are taken off the moor for breeding. And some settle down well enough in a new environment and come to trust people. I think Paddy is one of those."

Mrs Hope reached out and rubbed

Paddy's muzzle. Then she turned to the manager. "I'd like to blanket-saddle him and see if he'll let Paul mount him. Whoever rode him before obviously gave him a bad time. He might not like the idea of being ridden again."

The manager went off to fetch a thick blanket and a lightweight saddle. Mandy and Paul leaned on the fence and stroked Paddy again.

"It'll be OK, Paddy," Paul said quietly. "Where I used to go riding, they said I was very good at getting on to ponies' backs. And I'll be ever so gentle with you, I promise I will."

"You won't actually be able to ride Paddy yet, Paul," Mrs Hope told him. "It'll be a little while before he can be ridden. Those last few sores need to be completely cleared up first. But we'll see if Paddy will let you sit on him for a few minutes and maybe take a few steps. If he does, as long as you understand he'll need a lot of care and attention . . . well, I think maybe he could be a good pony for you."

"Oh, Mum, look at Paul's face! I wish we had a camera with us," said Mandy.

Paul was grinning so widely the corners of his lips nearly reached the straps of the riding hat the manager had insisted that he wore. He was sitting on a small saddle that had been placed over a soft, thick blanket on Paddy's back. And Paddy seemed more than happy for Paul to be there.

"OK, Paul," said the sanctuary manager, "I'll hold the leading rein and we'll just see if Paddy is willing to walk. Only a few paces, though," she added.

Paul clicked his tongue and whispered, "Walk on, Paddy!"

The pony didn't hesitate. And when Paul said "Whoa, boy," Paddy came to a gentle stop.

Smiling, the sanctuary manager lifted Paul down. They were both careful not

to touch Paddy's sore parts.

"Well done, Paul," said Mandy. "And well done, Paddy!"

Paul went round to Paddy's head and put his arms around the pony's neck. "They can't say no now!" he whispered. "You'll be coming home with me, Paddy. And soon you'll have lots of new friends. I know you're going to love everything."

"We wouldn't usually let a pony leave here while it still needed treatment," the sanctuary manager told Paul. "But I've talked it over with your mum and dad, and Mrs Hope says she'll show you exactly how to bathe Paddy's eyes and put the drops in, and how to put the special ointment on his sores. And she or Mr Hope will check Paddy over every few days."

"You can come and visit him any time you like," said Paul. "He'll have the best home a pony's ever had! Can we get him into the horse box now?"

At first, Paddy didn't want to go into the horse box. But when Paul ran up the ramp and called the pony, Paddy decided that he'd go in after all.

While Paul's parents were checking the box was firmly shut and locked, Mrs Hope looked down at Mandy. "I know you'd love to go back with them," she said. "But I think Paul should settle Paddy in on his own."

"OK, Mum," Mandy agreed. "I suppose you're right. Will it be OK if I say I'll call round to Jasmine Cottage tomorrow?"

"Yes. If it's all right with Paul's mum and dad, it's all right with me." Mrs Hope smiled and ruffled Mandy's hair.

5
The best of friends

When they got back to Animal Ark, Jean told Mandy that James had phoned. "Mrs Hunter's got a really bad cold so they're going to come home a day early," she explained. "They'll be home late tonight and James said to tell you he'll be round in the morning."

"Poor Mrs Hunter," said Mandy. "But it's great that James will be here tomorrow. I'll make a 'welcome home' card and go and put it through his letter-box. I don't want anyone to tell him about Paul and Paddy so I'll write an extra message on it. I'm going to tell him to come round as soon as he can in the morning and not to talk to anyone first!"

"Poor James." Mrs Hope laughed. "He'll be longing to find out what's going on when he reads that!"

James arrived at Animal Ark at half past eight. He was holding his welcome home card and he still looked half asleep. His brown hair was ruffled and the lace on one of his trainers hadn't been fastened.

"Welcome home, James!" Mandy said at once. "So much has happened while you were away!"

James asked what her mysterious message meant.

"I have a surprise for you," Mandy

replied. "But it's not here," she added, with a mischievous grin. "We'll have to go somewhere first."

It didn't take them long to cycle to Jasmine Cottage. Paul was waiting for them at the gate. "I've just phoned Animal Ark," he said. "Your dad told me you were on your way, Mandy. He's coming round to see Paddy later. Is this James?"

"Yes it is." Mandy quickly introduced the two boys. "James came home a day early, Paul. I knew you wouldn't mind him coming round with me."

"Have you told him about Paddy? Have you asked him about teaching me to whistle?" asked Paul.

"Mandy hasn't told me anything yet," said James, more confused than he already was. "Only that she's got a surprise for me," he continued. "But you mentioned me teaching you to whistle. So . . . I guess the surprise is a dog. A dog called Paddy!"

Paul grinned. "Come on, let's go and see him. He's in the paddock."

"Oh!" said James when they reached the paddock. "Paddy's a *pony*! He's . . . he's . . ." James glanced at Mandy and she knew her friend was disturbed at the pony's ragged appearance.

"Paul got Paddy from the Horse and Pony Rescue Sanctuary," Mandy said, explaining everything to James.

"He's going to need a lot of looking after to get him really well again," Paul added. "And Mandy said you'd both help me."

"Of course we will," said James shoving his glasses further on to his nose.

"Can you get Paddy to come to us, Paul?" asked Mandy. "We can introduce him to James, then."

"I'm not sure," Paul replied. "We tried to put him in his stable last night, but he didn't want to go in. So we let him stay out in the paddock. When I called him this morning he wouldn't come to me. I think he thought I was going to take him to the stable again.

"He lets *me* go to *him*," Paul continued, "and doesn't run off. But he doesn't seem to want to move from the middle of the paddock. I really want to see if Paddy will let me groom him."

"The paddock's a good place to do that," said Mandy. "Let's go and get his brushes!"

Paddy whinnied loudly as the three of them made their way across the paddock. "And he's swishing his tail!" said Mandy. "That's a good sign. I think he's pleased to see us."

Paddy *was* pleased to see them. He lay his big broad head on each shoulder in turn and even tried to lick James's glasses!

After they'd petted and stroked Paddy for a while, Paul ran a dandy-brush gently over the pony's body. "You're supposed to use a circular movement with this brush really," he said. "Then the stiff bristles remove any dirt. But I just want

him to get used to the feel of the different brushes first."

"Good idea," said Mandy, nodding. She picked up another brush and started to brush Paddy's mane. Then, while Paul brushed the pony's tail, James ran a soft brush over Paddy's ribs.

"Poor Paddy," said James. "He's very thin, isn't he? Look at his sticky-out ribs! And his coat needs some work."

"We'll soon have him looking right," said Mandy, kissing Paddy's muzzle, then laughing as Paddy blew hard down his nostrils.

Mr Hope said exactly the same thing when he came to check Paddy over: "Lots of loving, plenty of grooming, careful attention to his eye and his sores, a small helping of barley and linseed mash for his breakfast every day, halibut liver oil and malt at midday, plus his usual feed. All that, and you'll soon have him looking right."

"He won't go into his stable, Mr Hope," said Paul. "Will he be OK if we leave him out at night?"

"Yes, he'll be fine, Paul. And by the time it's winter, Paddy will be really used to you and his new home. By then, he'll probably look forward to going in his stable at night."

The next few days passed quickly. Mandy and James spent most of the time with

Paul and Paddy. James managed to teach Paul to whistle, and Paddy began to trot up to Paul whenever he heard the sound! Paul couldn't whistle at Paddy when Blackie was there, though, because the gangly-legged Labrador kept jumping up at him and making him laugh!

Mandy had been a bit worried the first time James brought Blackie with him. She'd read in one of her parents' animal care books that Exmoors were sometimes nervous of dogs. But Paddy and Blackie rubbed noses and were the best of friends right from the start!

Jane Jackson brought Paul a large white silk scarf. "If you put it over Paddy's soft grooming brush every time you use it, his coat will soon start to shine," she told Paul.

Paddy was looking better every day. He was still underweight and his scars hadn't faded much more, but his eye wasn't so swollen and his sores were almost completely healed.

One morning, Paul decided to surprise Mandy and James. He put Paddy on a leading rein and walked him down to the end of the lane to meet them. "It will get him used to the area for when I can ride him," he told them.

"And to the sound of traffic from the road into the village," Mandy added, rubbing her cheek over Paddy's soft muzzle.

"Paddy really likes walking along the lane," James said. "See how he's looking around, as if he's saying 'hello' to every tree and bush."

"And to every clump of grass." Paul laughed as the pony lowered his head and started to graze. "But I don't really like him eating this grass. Too many traffic fumes on it."

"I've brought him a carrot," said James. "That will distract him." He offered Paddy the carrot and Blackie woofed indignantly. "OK, OK." James laughed. "I've got a treat for you, as well."

The three friends spent the whole morning grooming Paddy in the paddock. Mandy's gran popped in to see them and invited them to lunch. "Not you, Paddy," she said. "You can have yours here. I've brought you some more carrots and a nice sweet apple."

They all had things to do after lunch. Mandy was going to the dentist, Mrs Hunter was taking James to visit relations and Paul's mum was taking him into Walton to have his hair cut ready for starting school. But Mrs Stevens said there was just time for Paul to walk Paddy to the end of the lane to see Mandy and James off.

"I can't believe we go back to school tomorrow," said Mandy as they walked along. "The time's gone really quickly since you got Paddy, Paul."

"I'm looking forward to coming to your school," Paul replied. "But I hope people are friendly."

"Oh, they will be, Paul. Wait and see

– you'll soon have loads of friends."

They were almost at the end of the lane when Paddy lowered his head and tried to nibble at the grass on the verge again.

"No, Paddy!" Paul said sternly. "You are *not* to do that!"

Mandy and James watched as Paul tried to make Paddy lift his head. "You're a naughty pony!" Paul said. He *sounded* cross, but Mandy and James could tell he was trying not to laugh. At last, Paul managed to persuade Paddy to stop nibbling.

Further up the lane on the other side, Mandy saw a lady and a girl standing still and staring hard at them.

Mandy recognised the girl. It was Tina Cunningham. She was in James's class at school. She was just about to wave when Tina and her mum turned and carried on up the lane.

Mandy didn't think any more about it. She and James said goodbye to Paul

and Paddy, then hurried off.

"Why does today feel different?" Mandy murmured when she woke up the next morning. Then she realised why: the summer holidays were over. She was going back to school!

"It'll be great to see my school-friends again and talk about what we've all done in the holidays," Mandy said over breakfast.

"Don't get talking so much that you forget about Paul," Mrs Hope reminded her with a smile.

"Don't worry, Mum," Mandy replied. "James and I aren't cycling to school today. We're meeting Paul at the end of his lane, so when we get to school we'll introduce him to all our friends and help him settle in. James is going to ask Mrs Black if he can take Paul round school to show him where everything is."

Mandy ran to get her coat and back-pack. Then she said goodbye and dashed off to meet James and Paul.

Paul was a few minutes late. "I had to explain to Paddy why I wouldn't be seeing much of him today," he said. "I really didn't want to say goodbye."

"There's still plenty of time," Mandy said. "There just won't be as *much* time to talk to everybody before the bell goes."

When the three of them walked into the playground, Mandy saw her friend Carrie. "Come on," said Mandy. "Here's someone I think you'll like."

But Carrie didn't seem very friendly, and she didn't even *look* at Paul when Mandy tried to introduce him!

Then Sarah Drummond walked past without speaking. She was in Mandy's class but she usually talked quite a lot to James. Sarah's Labrador, Sooty, was from the same litter as Blackie. Normally she would ask James how Sooty's brother was getting on.

When Mandy saw Jill Redfern and asked how Toto, her tortoise, was, Jill mumbled something and then hurried away. And three of the juniors – Susan Davis, Laura Baker and Jack Gardiner – who usually loved chatting to Mandy and James, ran off when they saw Mandy, James and Paul walking towards them.

Mandy couldn't understand it. It couldn't be because Paul was a new boy! Usually, everyone at Welford Primary School thought it was great when someone new started there. They would at least come over and say hello!

Just then Amy Fenton arrived. "Gosh!" she said, dashing up to Mandy. "I made it before the bell. I thought I was going to be really late. Minnie got out of her cage and it took me ages to catch her and put her back in."

Mandy laughed. Maybe she was just imagining that the others had been acting strangely. Amy was certainly friendly enough. "Minnie is Amy's mouse," she told Paul.

"And this is Paul Stevens," James told

Amy. "He's come to live in Jasmine Cottage near Mandy's grandparents."

"Hi, Paul!" Amy smiled. "Have *you* got any pets?"

The bell went before Paul could reply, and everyone made a mad dash to line up ready for going inside. James took Paul with him and stood behind him.

James was surprised to feel someone poking him hard in the back and to hear a fierce whisper: "You and Mandy Hope should be ashamed of yourselves!"

He swung round to see Tina Cunningham glaring scornfully at him. There was no time to ask Tina what she meant; the second bell rang and they all went inside and into their classrooms.

6

A terrible mistake

When Mandy got to her classroom, she began to feel uneasy again. Nobody called out to her to go and sit next to them. Nobody asked her what she'd done in the holidays or told her what they'd done. And when she walked over to look at Terry and Jerry, the class gerbils, she was almost sure she heard someone say that Terry and Jerry had better watch out!

Mandy was really glad when it was time to go into assembly. Then she'd be able to sit next to James and try to figure out why everyone was being so unfriendly.

But James didn't seem to want to talk, either. When Mandy hurried over to sit next to him, he stared straight ahead with a really serious look on his face. Mandy leaned forward to look at Paul, who was sitting next to James. Paul's shoulders were hunched and he was staring down at his feet. Had she done something wrong?

Amy Fenton was on Mandy's other side. Mandy turned her head to say something to her. But Amy whispered, "I wish I'd never spoken to you, Mandy. I'm so surprised!" Amy stopped whispering as Mrs Garvie, the Headteacher, stepped on to the platform.

Mandy usually enjoyed Mrs Garvie's start of term talks. But today she didn't hear a single word! She was too busy wondering what on earth was going on.

At break, Mandy tried to find James. Maybe he had some explanation for why everyone was ignoring her. But she couldn't see him anywhere. Paul was in the playground, though, and he walked slowly towards her.

"I hate your school, Mandy. You told me it was the best ever! But it isn't. Nobody wants to be friends with me. They won't even *talk* to me. I wish we'd never come to live in Welford. I hate it here!"

Before Mandy could say anything to try and comfort Paul, he dashed away and disappeared into the boys' washroom. Wasn't there anyone who would talk to her?

At lunch-time, James came up to Mandy. "I needed to see you without Paul being here," he said quickly. "I don't know what's going on, Mandy, but whatever

it is I'm sure it's something to do with Paul!"

Mandy nodded. "Maybe you're right, James. We've got to find out what it is and try and make things OK."

"We sure have!" James nodded fiercely and his glasses slid down his nose. "But I don't know how! Except . . ." he added thoughtfully. He told Mandy what Tina Cunningham had said to him earlier on. "But I've no idea what she was talking about!"

"So we go and ask her what she meant," Mandy said determinedly. "Look, there she is, over there with some of the others."

Mandy went straight over to where Tina and her friends were standing. But she didn't even get a chance to confront Tina.

"You and James should be ashamed of yourselves, Mandy Hope!" Tina began, as soon as Mandy was within earshot. "None of us can understand how you can talk to someone who's so cruel to his pony! I saw how badly that pony's being treated!"

Just at that moment, Paul came up. Tina pointed at him and continued loudly. "And I saw how *that* boy wouldn't let the pony eat the grass when the poor thing is so thin you can see its bones sticking out! He shouldn't be allowed to keep a pony. I told them all about it at the stables when I went for my riding lesson. They said I should report it to someone!"

Paul took a couple of steps towards Tina. "You've got it wrong!" he said. "Paddy is—"

"Paddy?" scoffed Tina. "More like *Patchy*, if you ask me. That pony is a mess!"

Paul made a strange gasping noise. Then, sobbing loudly, he ran off. He was running so quickly Mandy didn't think she'd be able to catch up with him. She was probably too cross to have tried to stop him anyway.

She marched up to Tina and stood squarely in front of her. "Now just you listen to me, Tina Cunningham!" Mandy's voice trembled with anger as she continued. "Paul's pony came from the rescue sanctuary. He'd been so badly treated by his previous owner that the sanctuary manager thought he'd have to stay there forever. Paddy didn't want to be friends with anyone until he saw Paul! And Paul really had to persuade everyone to let him have Paddy! I know how hard

that was, because I was there . . . and so
was my mum!"

Then James joined in and told everyone
how Paul spent all his time with Paddy,
grooming him, caring for him, giving him
special food, and putting special drops
into his eye twice a day.

"Paul's trying to make up for what
Paddy's previous owner did to him!"
Mandy explained. "And the reason he
wouldn't let Paddy eat that grass, Tina,
was in case it was covered in petrol fumes!

So now you know," Mandy added more quietly. "And I hope all of you feel really bad for how unhappy you've made Paul feel today. Now I'm going to try and find him!"

But Mandy and James couldn't find Paul. They searched everywhere they could think of. Then they decided to go back inside the school and look.

"I suppose, in a way, I can understand how Tina made such a terrible mistake," Mandy said as she and James went inside. "You and I have got so used to Paddy that we don't notice how thin and patchy he looks!"

James nodded. "*We* just notice that he looks better every day," he agreed.

Mrs Garvie saw them walking along the corridor. "I've just had a message from Mrs Stevens," she said gently. "Paul has gone home. His mother said she'll be keeping him there for the rest of the day. She asked me to ask both of you if you'd go round after school." She smiled kindly at them. "Do you know what happened to upset Paul?"

Mandy nodded. "We do, Mrs Garvie. But it was all a terrible mistake. I think things will be much better for Paul when he comes to school tomorrow," she added.

"I just hope we can make *Paul* believe that!" said James.

When James and Mandy went round to Jasmine Cottage after school, Paul wouldn't come and talk to them.

"Tina and the others understand about Paddy now," Mandy told Paul's mother. "We're almost sure everything will be fine at school in the morning."

"I'll tell him later on," said Mrs Stevens. "He's still very upset at the moment."

"Please could you phone me later to let me know how he is?" Mandy asked.

"Yes, I'll do that, Mandy." Mrs Stevens nodded.

★

Later that evening, Mrs Stevens phoned Mandy and told her Paul was feeling a bit happier about things. "I think his dad and I have managed to convince him that things will be better at school now," she said. "I reckon he'll be at the end of the lane to meet you and James in the morning."

"That's good," said Mandy. "I'll phone James and tell him."

7

Apologies

"What shall we do if Paul doesn't come?" Mandy asked worriedly as soon as she met up with James the next morning.

"I don't know," James answered.

They needn't have worried, though. When they got to Paul's lane he was already waiting for them. "Tina

Cunningham phoned me last night to say she was sorry for making such a terrible mistake," he explained. "I still don't feel too good about coming to school," Paul added as they walked along. "But Dad said it would be like letting Paddy down if I didn't."

Mandy smiled. She thought Mr Stevens had said exactly the right thing!

But as they walked through the school gates, she noticed how white Paul's face had gone, and she was sure his hands were screwed into tight, worried balls inside his pockets.

When the lining-up bell rang, Mandy and James were surprised to see Mrs Todd and Mrs Black come out of the building and walk over to stand with their classes.

They were even more surprised when, after the second bell rang, the teachers led the two classes round to the front door of the school. There was a lot of giggling and whispering and breaking out of line, and nobody got told off! Mandy and James couldn't understand it at all. Until they got into the main hall . . .

Then they saw a huge poster on the school's bulletin board. It said:

Good luck to Paul Stevens and Paddy!
And to Mandy Hope and
James Hunter, who are helping Paul
to make Paddy better.

There was a border of horseshoes all around the edges of the poster. Everybody from both classes had drawn one and written their name inside it – even the teachers.

"After you'd told us all about Paul and Paddy, we all felt really bad," Tina Cunningham explained. "Then we got the idea of doing the poster to show how sorry we were. We went to Mrs Black and Mrs Todd and told them everything!"

"The school secretary phoned our parents and we all stayed late after school to do it," said Amy Fenton.

"It was an excellent idea!" Mandy laughed. "And the poster's brilliant, too!"

"It sure is," agreed James.

Paul asked if he could take the poster home to put up in Paddy's stable. "And you're all welcome to come and see Paddy sometime," he added.

When everybody yelled "Great!" and "You bet!" Mandy was so happy for Paul. She knew he'd found lots of friends in Welford.

At first break, Paul showed Mandy the presents he'd found by his place in the classroom. "Apples, carrots, a pony magazine, a hoof-pick and a bar of saddle soap!" he told her happily. "And Tina Cunningham's going to ask her mum if she can come home with me after school tomorrow. We're going to polish all Paddy's tack ready for when I can ride him!"

"That's great, Paul!" said Mandy. It would be nice if Tina and Paul became good friends, she thought. After all, Tina really cared about ponies, too!

So Paul settled down well. He had to give his new friends a progress report on Paddy every day. And Paddy was doing just fine!

Early one Saturday morning, three weeks later, Mrs Hope answered the phone to hear an anxious-sounding Paul asking if she could come and look at Paddy. "He's acting really strangely," said Paul. "I'm worried that he's got tummy ache."

"I'll be with you in ten minutes, Paul." Mrs Hope put the phone down and called to Mandy.

"Do you think it's serious, Mum?" asked Mandy as she scrambled quickly into the Land-rover.

"I don't know, love. Paul certainly sounded very worried. But we'll just have to wait and see."

When they arrived at Jasmine Cottage, Mrs Stevens and Paul were standing by the paddock gate watching Paddy. "Look at him, Mrs Hope!" said Paul, pointing to the pony.

Paddy, his dark tail stuck straight out behind him, was galloping round and round the paddock. Every so often, he slowed down a bit and gave a funny little jump in the air. Then he was off again, galloping at a tremendous pace.

"He was doing that when I first came outside and he hasn't stopped since," Paul explained. "He won't come when I whistle for him, or when I call him."

"Does that mean he hasn't had his breakfast yet?" asked Mrs Hope. Paul nodded. Mrs Hope continued. "That's OK, then, I wouldn't have felt too happy about the way he's acting if he'd eaten right beforehand. Try calling him again and see what happens."

Mandy glanced thoughtfully at her mum. She didn't sound particularly worried.

"Paddy! Paddy!" called Paul. "Come on, boy. There's a good pony."

Mandy added her voice to Paul's. Suddenly, Paddy stopped and gave a low whinny. Then he drew in his nose until it touched his chest, and stretched first one hindleg, then the other, out behind him. He tossed his broad head, then trotted towards the paddock gate.

Mrs Hope smiled down at Paul. "I think Paddy has suddenly realised just how well he's feeling," she said. Paddy whinnied again and wrinkled

his muzzle as he got up close.

Mrs Hope rubbed his nose, then felt inside his mouth and ears and looked in his eyes. She climbed over the gate and stroked him all over his body and down his legs, her fingers feeling for any sign of pain or tension. Then she took a close look at his scars and the healed-up sores. "He's fine, Paul. Nothing to worry about at all."

"Oh dear," said Mrs Stevens. "So we called you out for nothing!"

"No problem," Mrs Hope told her. "Paddy was due for a visit from us today, anyway. But I think perhaps . . ." Mrs Hope smiled at Paul again, ". . . Paddy could be feeling a bit bored. It's time to give him a bit more to do during the day."

Paul looked at her, puzzled. But Mandy gave an excited squeak. She'd guessed what her mum was getting at.

"I mean, time for you to start thinking about riding Paddy!" Mrs Hope told Paul.

"I would begin by just putting his saddle and bridle on two or three times today, to get him used to you doing it and to the feel of them. Then tomorrow you could ride him gently around the paddock for a while."

"Wow!" said Paul. "That's terrific news!"

"Meantime," said Mrs Hope, "give Paddy a little bit of hay to nibble at before you let him have his proper feed. He'll be hungry after all that activity and might eat his food too quickly. Then he *could* get tummy ache."

"That's why I never give Paddy very cold water," said Paul. "In case that hurts his tummy."

"You're doing everything right, Paul!" Mrs Hope reassured him. "You've only had Paddy a little over a month, but the difference in him is amazing."

"Well, I've had lots of help from everybody," said Paul. "And," he added, looking at Mandy. "I think I'm going to need more help saddling him up for the first time and . . . getting on him tomorrow to ride him! I feel really nervous about it all."

"I'm sure you'll be fine," said Mrs Hope. "Just take everything nice and easy."

"I'll go and get Paddy's grooming stuff," said Paul. "We could phone James and ask him to come over as well, Mandy. You *are* staying, aren't you?"

Mandy looked at her mum. "It's all right by me." Mrs Hope nodded. "Don't be late for lunch, though. We're meant to be going shopping this afternoon, remember."

8

Ups and downs

"I just know I'm going to be all fingers and thumbs!" said Paul. He'd spent the last hour checking Paddy's tack and now he was about to saddle him. "It's ages since I saddled a pony," he added.

"You'll be OK, Paul," encouraged James. "I think Paddy understands what's happening. He's standing nice and still for you."

"He *is*!" agreed Mandy, climbing on to the middle rung of the gate and hanging over it to get a closer look.

Paddy moved his head forward to see what Paul was holding. He stretched his top lip away from his mouth.

"He's using his lip to feel the reins," Paul explained. "Is it OK if I put them on you, Paddy?"

Paul's fingers trembled slightly as he slipped the reins over Paddy's head and neck. But Paddy stood so patiently that Paul was soon handling everything with confidence. The pony didn't even mind when Paul slipped a thumb into the side of his mouth to put the bit in.

"Now for the saddle, Paddy," said Paul. "There's a good pony. You are standing nice and quiet, aren't you?"

Paul stepped back to look proudly at the saddled pony. "I'll only keep it on for a few minutes this time," he said. "I'll leave it on for longer after lunch."

"Hold it there!" Mr Stevens spoke quietly as he came up behind James and Mandy and started clicking a camera. "I think you and James ought to be in a photo too, Mandy," he said. "Hop over the gate and go and stand next to Paul and Paddy."

After they'd had their photo taken it was time for Mandy and James to go. But they promised Paul they'd be back the next day to watch his first proper ride!

★

"Well, here goes," said Paul, sounding nervous. He stroked Paddy's neck, then turned so he was standing with his back to the pony's head. He took the reins in his left hand and placed them just in front of the saddle. He took hold of the saddle with his right hand and put his left foot in the stirrup.

"I'm scared to do it!" said Paul, taking his foot out of the stirrup.

Paddy gave a small whinny and swung his head round to gaze at Paul.

"There! Paddy's telling you not to be so silly!" said Paul's mum. "He wants you to ride him. Just look how bright his eyes are!"

"OK, OK," muttered Paul, stroking Paddy's cheek before gently pushing the pony's head away. "I'll do it this time, Paddy. I promise."

Paul took a deep breath and put his foot in the stirrup again. This time, he followed through. He beamed down at

James and Mandy from Paddy's back, then spoke quietly to his pony and, the next minute, Paddy was 'walking on'. After a few turns around the paddock, Paul called, "I'm going to get him to trot."

Mandy heard running footsteps behind her and turned to see who was coming. It was Jane Jackson. "I was on my way home and I saw Paul and Paddy from the lane. I just *had* to come and watch!" she said.

"That pony moves really well," she added, her eyes following Paddy. "I wouldn't mind betting that he's a good little jumper. Has Paul ever done any jumping, Mrs Stevens?"

"He did a bit at the riding-school he went to before we came here," Mrs Stevens replied. "Perhaps we should set a few jumps up in the paddock," she added thoughtfully. "If Paul likes the idea, and if your mum thinks Paddy's fit enough, Mandy, we could plan it for next weekend!"

Paul loved the idea. And the next time

Mrs Hope checked Paddy over, she said he was definitely fit enough.

"Great!" said Paul. "Do you hear that, Paddy? On Saturday, we're going to try jumping. And don't worry, Mrs Hope," he added. "I won't let Paddy strain himself or anything. If he doesn't like it, we won't do it."

Mr Stevens bought some thick, round lengths of wood to use for poles and on Saturday morning Paul, Mandy, James and Jane helped him set up a series of wide-apart 'pole-jumps'. They placed each pole across two bricks about thirty centimetres off the ground.

Paul had tethered Paddy to the outside of the paddock gate and the pony kept whinnying loudly. "I'm sure he knows what this is all about!" said Paul. "Paddy's a very clever pony."

"Well, that's the last jump done," Jane told him. "Time to mount him, Paul. I'll hold the gate open for you when you're ready."

"I'll walk him round the outside of the jumps first," said Paul. "To make sure he sees them all and isn't frightened of them."

"Paddy certainly *isn't* frightened!" chuckled James. "He looks the way Blackie looks when I pick up his lead."

"Good job he doesn't leap up like Blackie, though!" Mandy joked.

Paul walked, then cantered Paddy up to each pole. Paddy soared over them easily. Jane had guessed right. Paddy *was* a really fine jumper.

"Paul's good, Mr Stevens," said Jane, after Paul and Paddy had been round the course several times. "Really good. Do you think he'd like to join our Pony Club up at the riding stables? Then he could enter the gymkhana I'm organising for the under-tens."

"I'm sure he'd love that." Mr Stevens nodded. "You ask him, Jane."

When Paul dismounted, he gave Paddy a big cuddle and told him what a good

pony he was. Paddy blew into Paul's face then rubbed his soft muzzle up and down his cheek. "I *know* you enjoyed it, Paddy!" said Paul. "But I'm going to unsaddle you now and you can have a rest."

Jane asked Paul about the gymkhana. "I could come round on Prince and we could have some mini-competitions in your paddock to get Paddy used to the idea," she said.

"I'd love you to bring Prince round," Paul said. "But I don't want to join the club or take part in a proper gymkhana, Jane."

"Whyever not, Paul?" asked Mr Stevens, sounding surprised.

"I just don't want to, that's all," mumbled Paul, turning red.

"OK." Jane sighed. "But we're having a sort of gymkhana practice tomorrow. Why don't you come up to the stables and meet the club members and their ponies, Paul?"

"The stables are awfully far away. It would be too far for Paddy just yet," said Paul.

"I'll drive you there," Mr Stevens told him.

"Thanks, Dad," said Paul. But he didn't sound very enthusiastic.

When Jane and his parents had gone, Paul glanced at Mandy and James and blurted out, "I'd love to join the club really. But Tina Cunningham told me they've got some really beautiful ponies there. Palominos and shiny, chestnut Welsh Mountain ponies. I love Paddy lots and lots, but I know he isn't beautiful. I'd hate it if anyone laughed at him or thought he looked patchy. Paddy wouldn't like it, either."

"But he doesn't look patchy any more, Paul!" said James, running his hand over Paddy's back.

"Maybe not. But his coat isn't sleek and shiny like Prince's. And it won't be as sleek as the other ponies' coats at the stable. I just know it." Paul shook his head. His answer was still "no".

A few days later, Jane came up to Mandy and James in the village when they were walking Blackie. "I can't understand why Paul won't join the club!" she said. "I've asked him over and over again! He seems really pleased when I take Prince round to compete against him and Paddy. I just know they'd have a marvellous time at the gymkhana."

"Maybe James and I can persuade him to join the club and to enter the gymkhana!" Mandy said determinedly. "Can't we, James?"

James nodded. But he wasn't too sure *how* they were going to do it.

"Make it soon then, Mandy," Jane said. "The entry forms have to be in by Friday. That only leaves you three days!"

By Hand

The Pony Club
Secretary

9

Problems for Mandy

When Mandy went home, she talked things over with her mum and dad.

"Paul's scared that the Pony Club members might laugh at Paddy!" she said. "We all think Paddy's gorgeous, but . . ."

"Paddy isn't as handsome as most ponies." Mr Hope nodded in agreement.

"But you know, Mandy, he *is* a perfect Exmoor."

"Is he?" Mandy asked thoughtfully. "Is he really, Dad?"

"Uh-oh!" Mrs Hope laughed. "I recognise that look on your face, Mandy Hope! What have you thought of?"

"Well, could one of you possibly find some excuse to call round at Paul's tomorrow afternoon and mention that? I think it could make a big difference to how Paul feels about Paddy."

The next day, Paul was just jumping Paddy over a double fence when Mr Hope arrived. He winked at Mandy and said he happened to be passing so he'd come to collect her. Mandy smiled happily. She could always count on her dad.

When Paul trotted over on Paddy, Mr Hope went into action. "You've worked wonders, Paul," he said. "Paddy's winter coat is going to be fantastic. It's thick and springy, and look at his tail!"

"This bit at the top looks like a fan," said Mandy.

"We call that an ice tail," Mr Hope told them. "In the native wild, on Exmoor, the tail gives protection against rain and snow. And Paddy's eyes are hooded for the same reason, aren't they, fella! You really *are* a perfect Exmoor."

"Did you hear that, Paddy?" murmured Mandy, planting a kiss on the pony's muzzle. "A *perfect* Exmoor! If you belonged to me, I'd want to show you off. I'd want everyone to see you!"

She looked at Paul. "I think it's a real shame you won't join the Pony Club!"

"Yup!" James agreed. "I'm sure none of the Pony Clubbers would laugh at a perfect Exmoor pony."

"Well, if he's as perfect as you say, maybe I will think about joining after all," said Paul.

"I think maybe ponies need *pony* friends as well as human ones!" Mandy said.

"That's right," added James. "Blackie enjoys being with other dogs. I bet Paddy would—"

"OK! OK! I'll do it!" said Paul, sliding quickly off Paddy's back. "I'll join the club *and* enter the gymkhana! Where do I get the forms from?"

"I bet Jane's got some!" said Mandy. "Have you got time to drive me up to Rose Cottage, Dad?"

"You could fill the forms in now, Paul, and one of us could post them for you on our way home," James said.

Mr Hope winked at Mandy once more. The plan had worked!

A little while later, Paul – helped by his mother, Mandy, James and Mr Hope – had filled in all the details on the forms. Mrs Stevens wrote out a cheque for the entry fee and addressed the envelope to the Pony Club Secretary.

Just then, Mr Hope's mobile phone rang. It was Mrs Forsyth, the owner of the riding stables. One of her ponies was giving birth to twin foals and needed a bit of help in delivering the second one.

"Do you want to come with me, Mandy?" Mr Hope asked.

Mandy nodded eagerly. "And I'll do better than *post* your entry form, Paul! The Pony Club's office is at the riding stables. I'll give the form to the secretary while Dad's helping with the second foal!"

When they arrived at the stables Mandy said she'd go to the Pony Club office with Paul's entry form right away. As Mandy walked, she stopped to talk to and stroke all the ponies who popped their heads over the half-doors of their stables. Their names were displayed on name-plates above the doors: Jet, Dixie, Megan, Jester, Smoky . . .

Smoky! Mandy thought. There was something strange about the beautiful grey pony. She seemed to be staring hard

at nothing, and she didn't blink or move when Mandy reached out to pet her.

"Your neck feels all tight, and it's damp and warm!" Mandy said worriedly.

Smoky's ears didn't flicker at all when Mandy spoke. They stayed forward and the pony just kept staring into space. "I think I'd better fetch somebody!" said Mandy. "Dad!"

"It looks like tetanus," Mr Hope said quietly, after he'd examined Smoky. "It's very serious, but hopefully we might just have caught it in time. I'm going to put cotton wool in her ears, because noise will upset her. I'll give her some injections and we need lots of bales of straw. We'll have to pack them all around her to stop her falling down. Move as quickly and as quietly as you can."

Mrs Forsyth, one of the stable lads and Mandy all fetched bales and helped surround Smoky with them.

"She won't want to eat," Mr Hope explained. "Chewing and swallowing will hurt too much. So try spoon-feeding her with water. I'll come back later and fix up a special drip."

"Will Smoky get better, Dad?" Mandy asked miserably, on their way home. "She looks very ill."

"She *is* very ill," Mr Hope said, nodding. "Mum or I will have to go and see her at least once a day. But I think she might make it," Mr Hope added.

★

Nearly a week went past before Mr Hope said he thought Smoky was out of danger. Mandy saw Jane Jackson that day and happily told her the good news.

"That's great!" Jane smiled. But then she frowned and said, "I thought you said you'd persuaded Paul to join the club and enter the gymkhana, Mandy. His name didn't appear in the list they published in the newspaper. Did he change his mind?"

Mandy's heart skipped a beat and her hand went to her mouth. She hadn't given the envelope to the secretary; she'd forgotten all about it! She didn't even know where she'd put it!

"I was on my way to the office with the entry forms when I saw Smoky acting strangely," she told Jane. "I must have put the envelope down somewhere when I ran for help, or when I was helping with the bales of straw. Perhaps I could go up to the riding stables and look for it. Or should I get Paul to fill in some more forms? Have you got any left?"

Jane looked worried. "It's a very strict rule that once the list of entrants has been published, no more names can be added to it," she explained.

"But Paul's name should have been on the list!" said Mandy. "He filled the forms in before the closing date. And he wrote the date on the forms. When I find the envelope, the secretary will see they were filled in on time. I'll be able to explain what happened!"

"I don't know if that would make any difference, Mandy!" Jane said. "But let's cycle up to the riding stables now. I'll help you explain everything to Miss Fletcher, the secretary. She just might be able to think of a way round things. She knows all about what happened to Smoky, so that should help!"

But it didn't help. Miss Fletcher said she was really, really sorry, but there was no way she could add Paul's name to the list of entrants – not now that the list had been in the paper. "But Mrs Stevens even wrote a cheque for the entry fee," said Mandy. "If I can just find the envelope—"

"I'm afraid Paul will have to wait for the next gymkhana," said Mrs Fletcher. "And you'd better explain what's happened to Mrs Stevens as quickly as possible, Mandy. She'll need to cancel the cheque she wrote."

"Don't worry, Mandy," said Jane. "I'll have a word with Mrs Stevens."

"I don't know *how* I'm going to tell Paul," Mandy said, as she and Jane cycled back to Welford. Her bike wobbled a bit as she lifted a hand to wipe away a tear. "I've really let him down."

"I'm sure Paul will understand," said Jane.

"But I feel like I've let Paddy down as well," said Mandy. She'd never felt so bad in all her life!

10

The gymkhana

"It doesn't matter, Mandy. *Really* it doesn't!" said Paul when Mandy told him what had happened. "Getting help for Smoky was more important than handing my entry forms in!"

"Yes, it was. But I should have remembered your forms afterwards!"

Mandy sighed unhappily.

"Listen, Mandy," said Paul. "I can still join the club. There's no problem there. And that's the important thing. Paddy will still be able to have the pony friends you talked about!"

Mandy nodded. But she still felt terrible.

James tried to think of ways to make her feel better. On the day before the gymkhana, he asked her to help him give Blackie a bath! Mandy wore her new wellies so Blackie couldn't make her feet all wet! And just for a little while Mandy didn't feel so bad. But then they took Blackie for a walk and they met Jane Jackson.

Jane told Mandy she was going to try to organise another gymkhana quite soon. "Maybe a special New Year one," she said.

"But New Year's ages away!" said Mandy. "Besides, it was *this* one that would have been so special for Paul."

"Why would it have been so special?" Jane asked gently.

Mandy gulped. "Well, even though Dad told Paul that Paddy's a perfect Exmoor pony, I'm sure Paul still worries about Paddy looking a bit different from other ponies. They'd have done well at the gymkhana. I'm sure they'd have won at least one prize."

James nodded. "And everyone would have clapped and cheered, and Paul would have been so proud of the pony he saved!"

"*James!*" shrieked Mandy. "You've just made me think of the most brilliant idea! We'll have to ask Dad about it first, and then make sure Paul comes to the gymkhana. Come on, we've got to go to Animal Ark!"

Mandy, Paul and James watched all the gymkhana events together. Mandy kept glancing anxiously round to see if her mum or dad had arrived.

Mr Hope had been chosen to give out the prizes at the end of the gymkhana.

He had been called out just before they'd left home, but told Mandy that he would definitely be back in time for prize-giving.

Now they were on the last event and Mandy couldn't see him anywhere!

"The strawberry roan pony is going to win," shouted Paul. "He's fantastic! I hoped he'd come first and . . . and . . . yes! He's done it!"

"And it'll soon be time for the prizes to be awarded," Mandy whispered to James, who was on her other side.

"Here's your dad now, Mandy!" said James a few minutes later. He pointed to a figure running hard across the field towards the bales of piled-up hay that were to be the presentation platform.

So the prize-giving began. There was lots of cheering and clapping and Mandy cheered loudest of all because she was so excited about what was going to happen at the end.

When the last winner had walked away with a rosette, Mr Hope stepped forward again and called for silence. "I now have a very special announcement to make and a very special rosette to present!"

He looked down to where Mandy, James and Paul were standing. Mandy's eyes sparkled as she gazed at her dad and she heard James take a deep, expectant breath.

"We have with us today," said Mr Hope, "somebody who's devoted a lot of time, care and attention – and *love* – to a pony who needed all those things more than most ponies do! I'm talking about Paul Stevens, who's given Paddy, a pony from the rescue sanctuary, a happy and loving home."

Mr Hope held up his hands to stop the applause. "Circumstances prevented Paul from entering the gymkhana," he said. "But I'd like Paul to come up to receive this special rosette because Paul's friends, especially Paddy, think he deserves a prize!"

Paul looked from Mandy to James in

astonishment. James thumped him on the back and Mandy laughed happily. Then she and James took hold of Paul's arms and propelled him to the platform to receive his rosette.

When the cheering died down, Jane Jackson stepped forward. "And I've also got a special announcement to make," she said. She beckoned to Paul.

Mr Hope reached under the table the prizes had been on. Smiling, he passed Jane a hard riding hat. Jane passed it to Paul.

Paul was puzzled. "But I've already got a riding hat," he said.

"It's *your* hat, Paul!" Jane told him. "Put it on, then go over to the ring."

Then Jane moved closer to the microphone. "Listen, everybody," she said. "Paul Stevens and Paddy are going to lead the other winners round the ring in a special Pony Parade! Go on, Paul!" she laughed. "Your mum and dad are waiting by the ring with Paddy!"

"They *can't* be," said Paul. "Paddy's in his paddock. I said goodbye to him just before I left to meet James and Mandy."

"They are, Paul. Truly!" said Jane. "Now, off you go. Or don't you want Paddy to have place of honour in the parade?" she added, teasingly.

"I can't believe it! I just can't believe it," said Paul as he, Mandy, James and Mr Hope walked towards the ring. "I mean, how did Paddy get here? We haven't got a horse box. Dad had to hire one when we went to the sanctuary."

"My dad borrowed one!" Mandy chuckled, squeezing Mr Hope's arm hard. "We fixed it all up yesterday afternoon!"

"I don't know what to say," said Paul, shaking his head. "I feel like I'm dreaming!"

"Paddy knows it's for real," said James, pointing to where the pony was standing with Mr and Mrs Stevens. "He's spotted you coming, Paul. He's pulling at the reins trying to get to you!"

Paul gave a loud whoop of joy and hurried forward to throw his arms round Paddy's neck. Then, grinning happily at his mum and dad, Paul fixed the rosette to Paddy's bridle.

A few seconds later they all watched as Paul mounted Paddy, then trotted him into the ring. As he got close to one of the Palomino ponies, Paddy stopped. He stretched his upper lip and used it to explore the Palomino's mane and ears.

"Look!" shouted someone in the

crowd. "That pony is smiling at the Palomino!"

Paul beamed round at everybody, patted Paddy, then said huskily, "Walk on, boy."

Paddy flicked his tail and walked on to take his place at the front of the parade.

Mandy felt so happy for Paul! James grinned at her, then jumped up and down with delight as everyone started clapping and cheering.

There were quite a few kids from school in the crowd. They set up a chant: "Paul and Paddy! Paul and Paddy! Paul and Paddy!" And before long everyone joined in the chant.

Paul smiled and waved and the chant became louder still. The pony clubbers riding behind Paul and Paddy halted their ponies and joined in. Paul laughed aloud and stroked Paddy's neck. He looked so proud of his pony!

Paul and Paddy will have even more new friends after today, thought Mandy

as she watched them go once round the ring on their own.

Then Paul called to the other riders to follow him and he urged Paddy into a brisk trot. This time, when Paul rode Paddy to where Mandy and James were standing, the Exmoor pony whinnied loudly.

Mandy gave an enormous, contented sigh. She was sure that whinny was just for them!

LUCY DANIELS
Animal Ark Pets

0 340 67283 8	Puppy Puzzle	£2.99	☐
0 340 67284 6	Kitten Crowd	£2.99	☐
0 340 67285 4	Rabbit Race	£2.99	☐
0 340 67286 2	Hamster Hotel	£2.99	☐
0 340 68729 0	Mouse Magic	£2.99	☐
0 340 68730 4	Chick Challenge	£2.99	☐
0 340 68731 2	Pony Parade	£2.99	☐

All Hodder Children's books are available at your local bookshop or newsagent, or can be ordered direct from the publisher. Just tick the titles you want and fill in the form below. Prices and availability subject to change without notice.

Hodder Children's Books, Cash Sales Department, Bookpoint, 39 Milton Park, Abingdon, OXON, OX14 4TD, UK. If you have a credit card you may order by telephone – (01235) 831700.

Please enclose a cheque or postal order made payable to Bookpoint Ltd to the value of the cover price and allow the following for postage and packing:
UK & BFPO – £1.00 for the first book, 50p for the second book, and 30p for each additional book ordered up to a maximum charge of £3.00.
OVERSEAS & EIRE – £2.00 for the first book, £1.00 for the second book, and 50p for each additional book.

Name ....

Address ....

....

....

If you would prefer to pay by credit card, please complete:
Please debit my Visa/Access/Diner's Card/American Express (delete as applicable) card no:

Signature ....
Expiry Date ....